BENJAMIN BEAR

in

BRAIN STORMS!

PHILIPPE COUDRAY

BENJAMIN BEAR

IN

BRAIN STORMS!

A TOON BOOK BY

PHILIPPE COUDRAY

A JUNIOR LIBRARY GUILD SELECTION

Also look for: **Benjamin Bear in Fuzzy Thinking**
Benjamin Bear in Bright Ideas!

The Benjamin Bear books have received the following accolades:

ALA NOTABLE CHILDREN'S BOOKS 2014
BOOKLIST'S TOP 10 GRAPHIC NOVELS FOR YOUTH 2014
A JUNIOR LIBRARY GUILD SELECTION 2013
ALA CHILDREN'S GRAPHIC NOVEL READING LIST 2013
EISNER AWARD BEST PUBLICATION FOR EARLY READERS NOMINEE 2012 & 2014
WINNER OF THE YOUNG READERS PANDA AWARD 2012-2013
NEW YORK PUBLIC LIBRARY'S 100 TITLES FOR READING AND SHARING 2011

For Michael, my best English teacher

Editorial Director: FRANÇOISE MOULY

Book Design: FRANÇOISE MOULY & JONATHAN BENNETT

Translation: FRANÇOISE MOULY

PHILIPPE COUDRAY'S artwork was drawn in India ink and colored digitally.

A TOON Book™ © 2015 TOON Books, an imprint of RAW Junior, LLC, 27 Greene Street, New York, NY 10013. Original French text and art © 2009-2013 Philippe Coudray and La Boîte à Bulles. No part of this book may be used or reproduced in any manner whatsoever without written permission except in the case of brief quotations embodied in critical articles and reviews. TOON Books®, TOON Graphics™, LITTLE LIT® and TOON Into Reading!™ are trademarks of RAW Junior, LLC. All rights reserved. All our books are Smyth Sewn (the highest library-quality binding available) and printed with soy-based inks on acid-free, woodfree paper harvested from responsible sources. Printed in Shenzhen, China by Imago. Distributed to the trade by Consortium Book Sales and Distribution, Inc.; orders (800) 283-3572; orderentry@perseusbooks.com; www.cbsd.com.

Library of Congress Cataloging-in-Publication Data:

Coudray, Philippe, author, illustrator.   Benjamin Bear in Brain storms! : TOON Level 2 / by Philippe Coudray.   pages cm. -- (Benjamin Bear)   Summary: "A collection of one-page comic strips featuring Benjamin Bear, a very serious bear who has his own silly logic for doing things"-- Provided by publisher.   ISBN 978-1-935179-82-5   1. Graphic novels. [1. Graphic novels. 2. Bears--Fiction. 3. Humorous stories.]   I. Title. II. Title: Brain storms! PZ7.7.C68Bc 2015 741.5'6944--dc23   2014028851

ISBN 978-1-935179-82-5 (hardcover)

15 16 17 18 19 20 IMG 10 9 8 7 6 5 4 3 2 1

Fetch

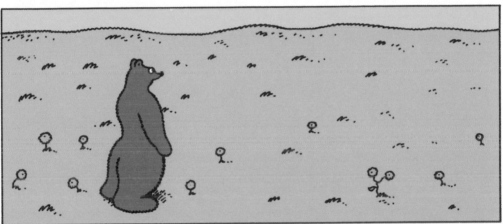

philippe Coudray

9

Solution

Philippe Coudray

The date

Philippe Coudray

The big tree

Philippe Coudray

12

The cliff

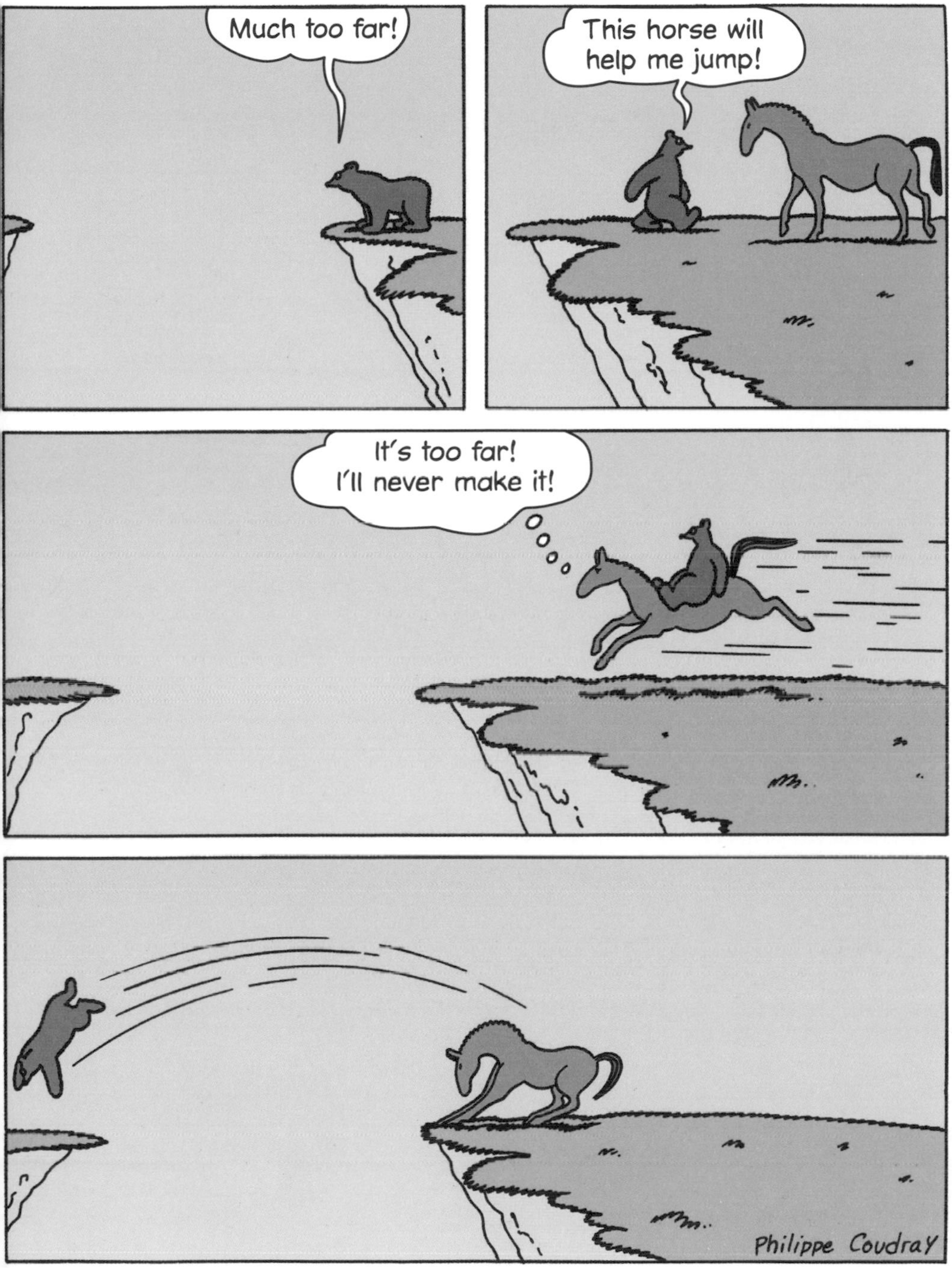
Much too far!
This horse will help me jump!
It's too far! I'll never make it!
Philippe Coudray

Heavy lifting

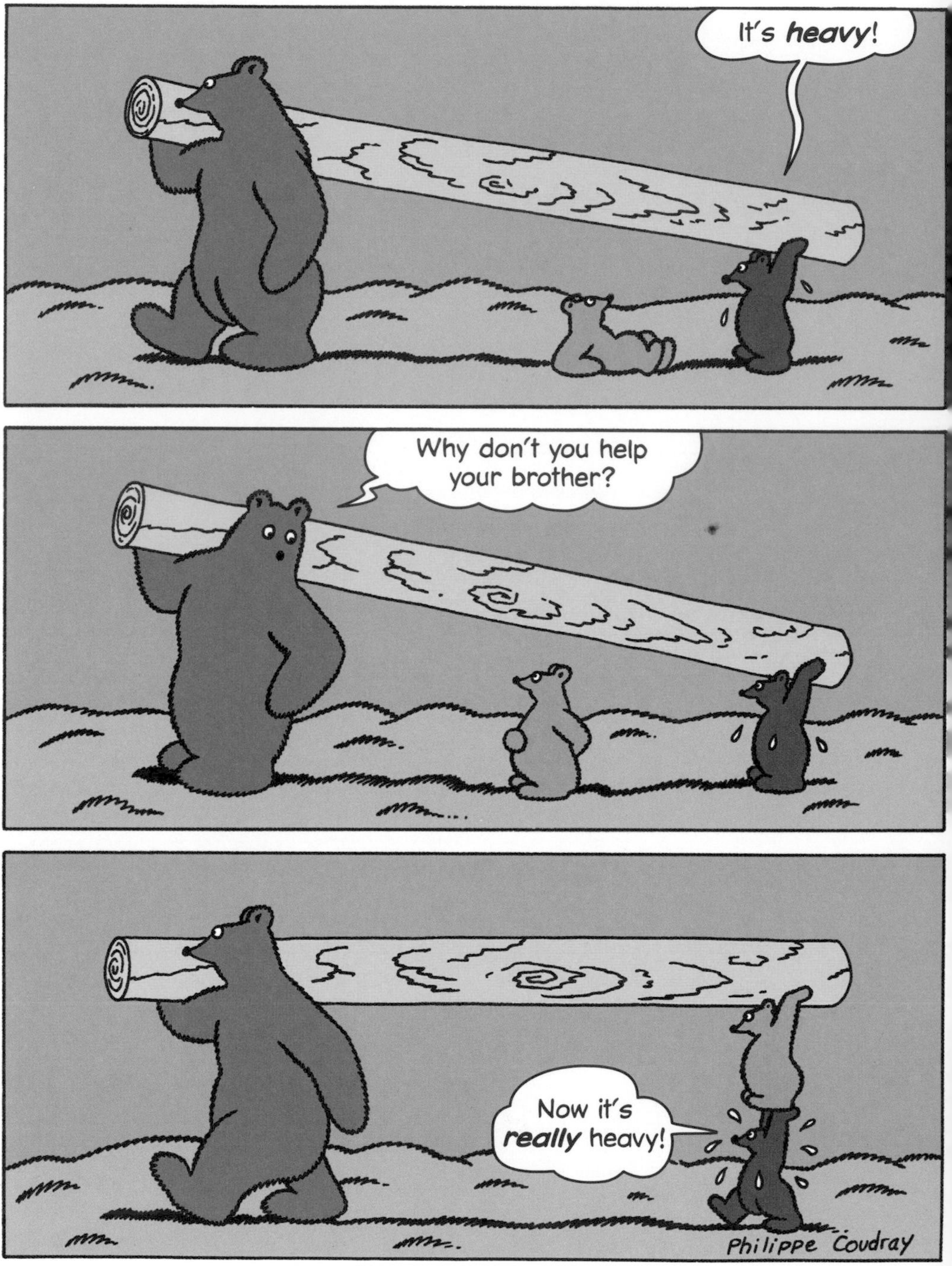
It's **heavy**!
Why don't you help your brother?
Now it's **really** heavy!
Philippe Coudray

The target

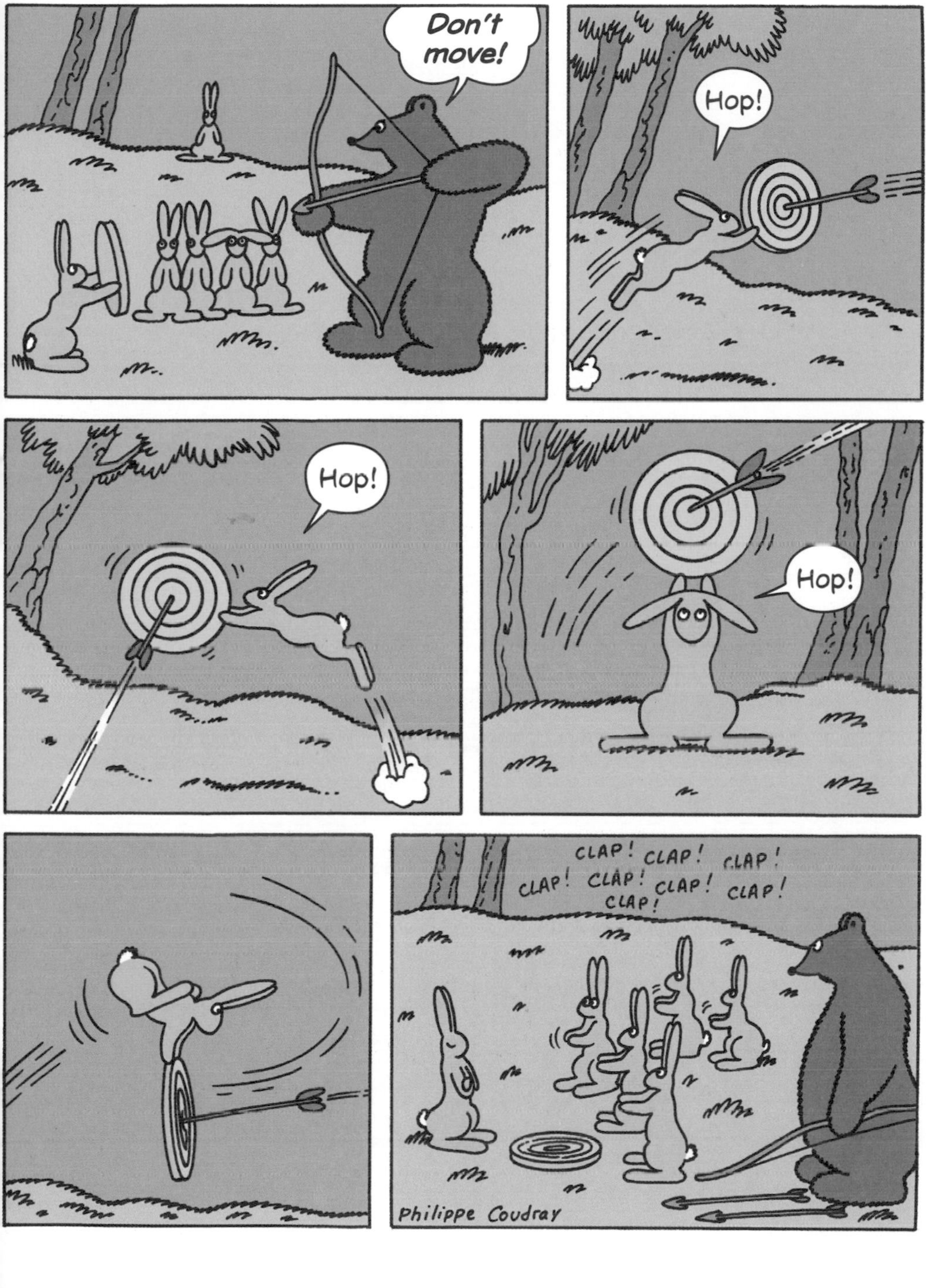
Don't move!
Hop!
Hop!
Hop!
CLAP! CLAP! CLAP!
CLAP! CLAP! CLAP! CLAP!
CLAP!
Philippe Coudray

Math lesson

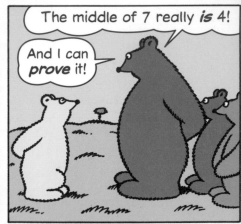

Philippe Coudray

16

Patience

Philippe Coudray

17

Snow

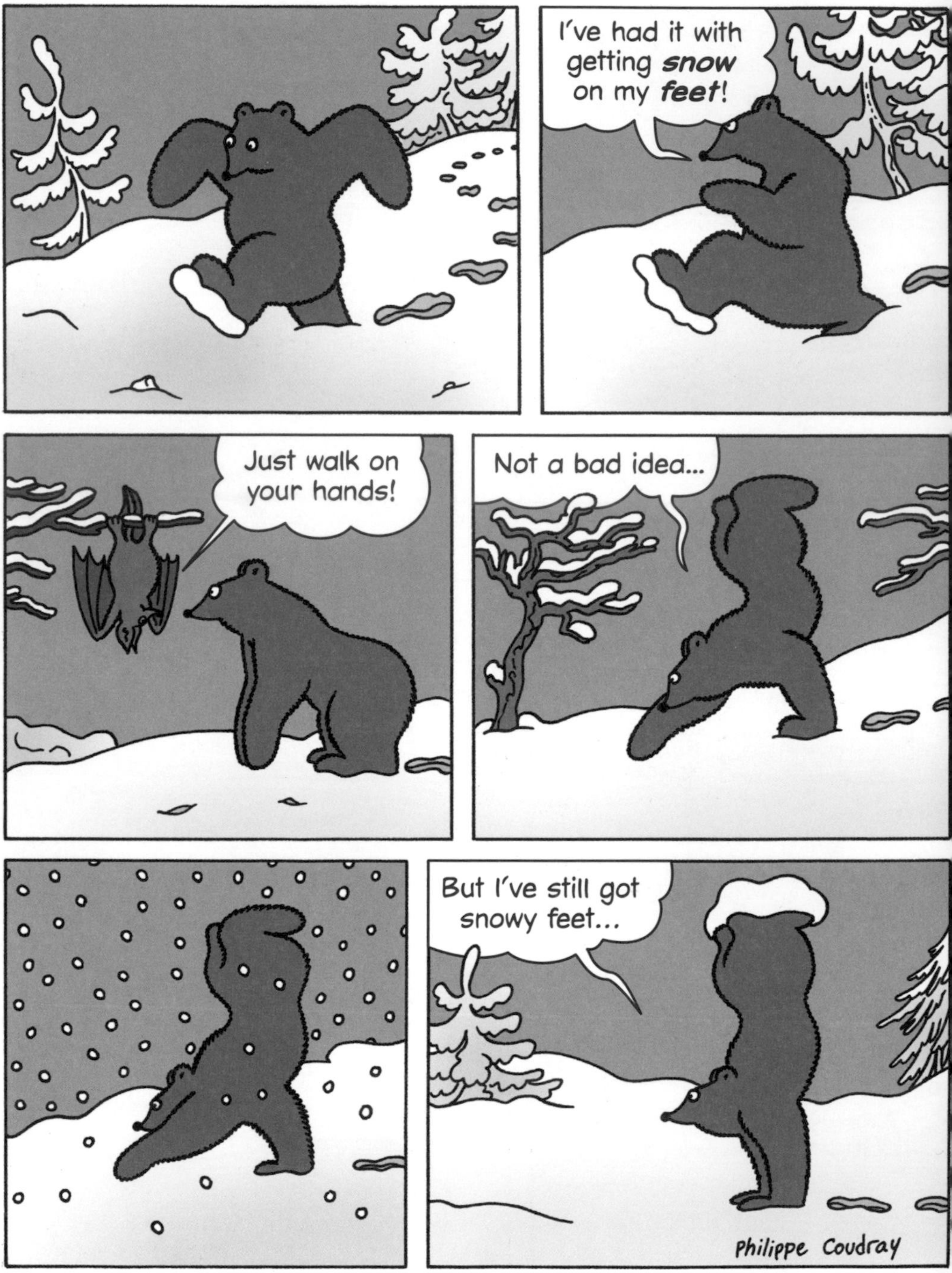
I've had it with getting ***snow*** on my ***feet***!
Just walk on your hands!
Not a bad idea...
But I've still got snowy feet...
Philippe Coudray

Ski group

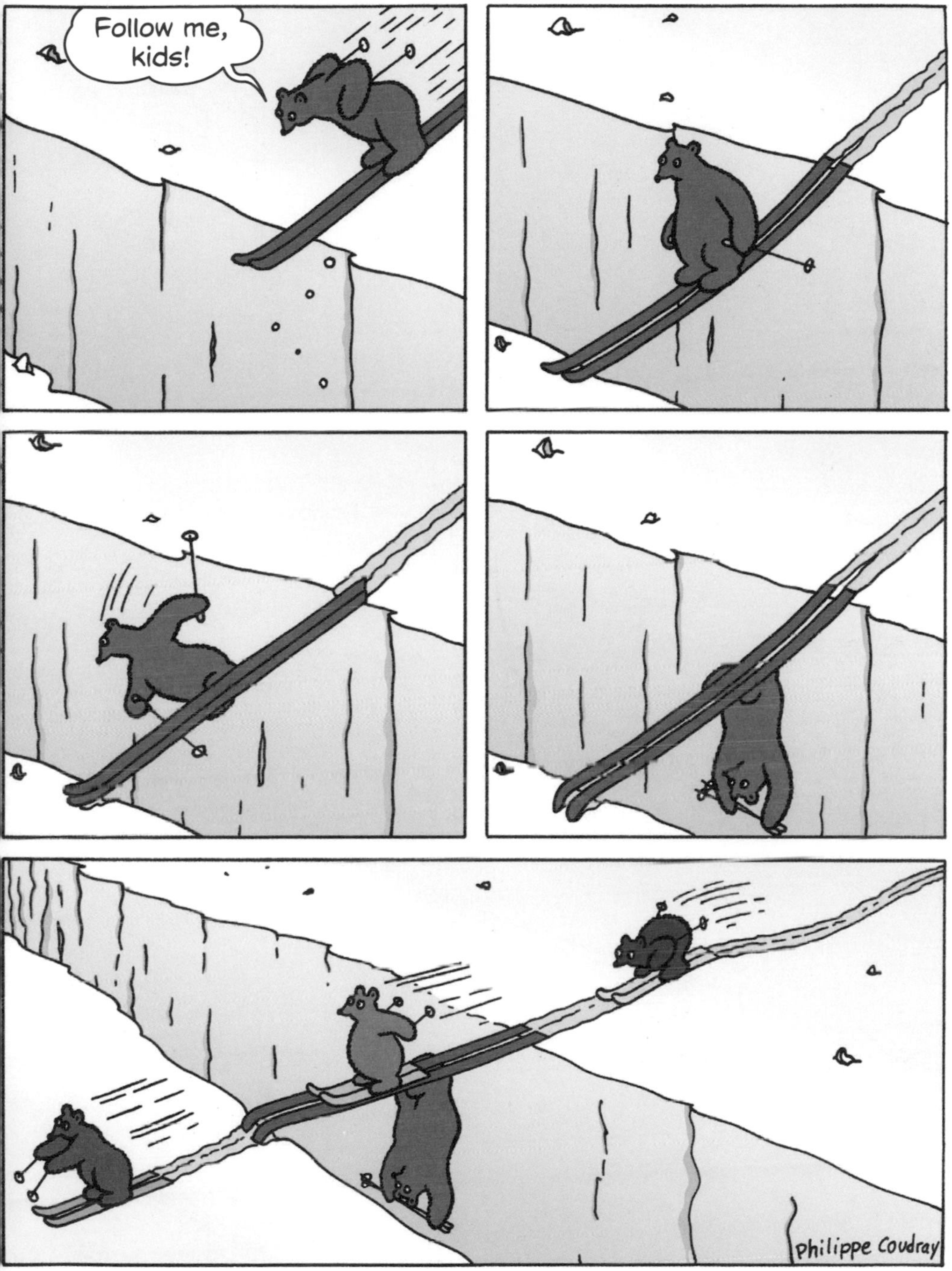
Follow me, kids!
Philippe Coudray

Canvas

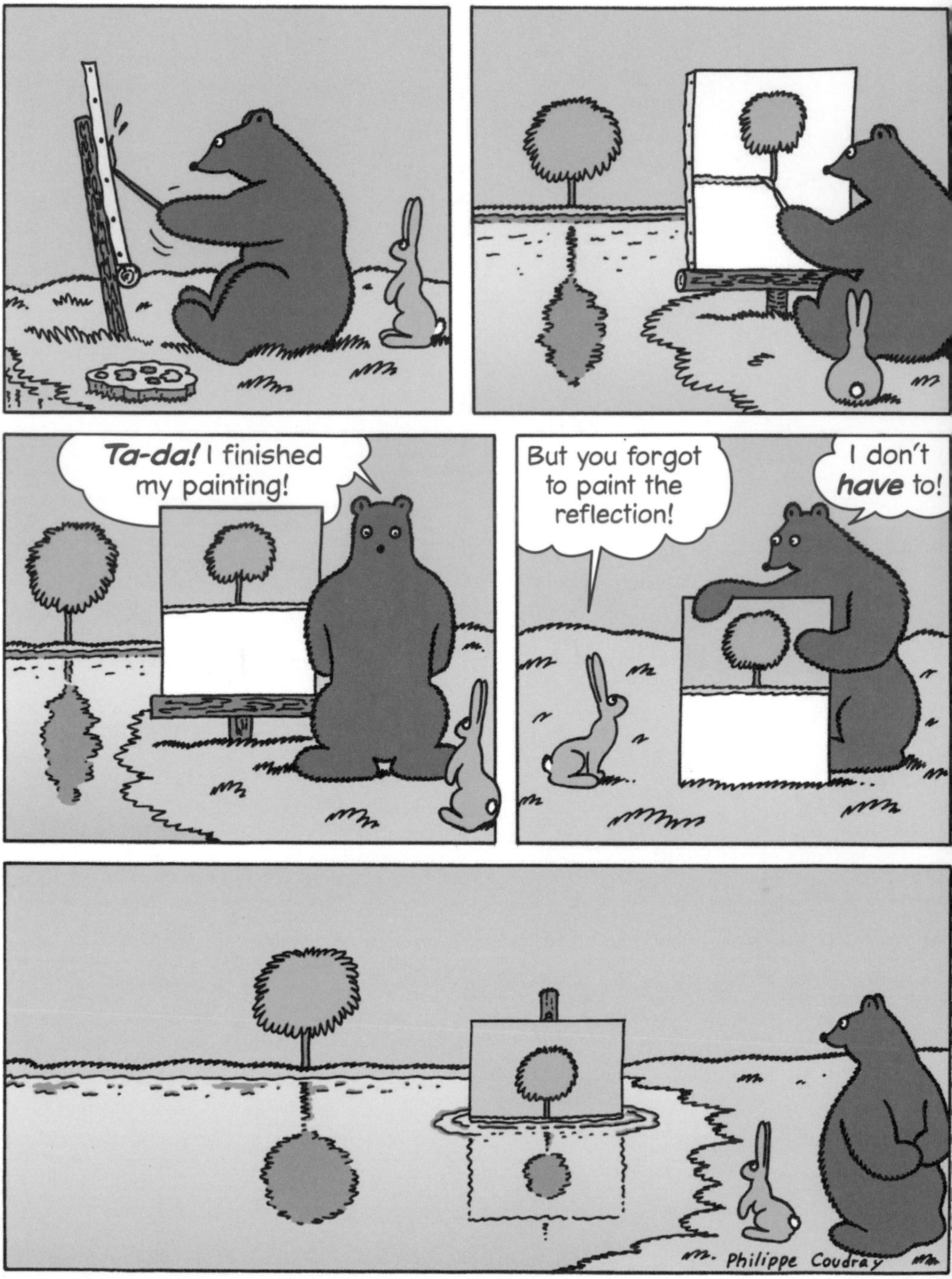

Ta-da! I finished my painting!
But you forgot to paint the reflection!
I don't have to!
Philippe Coudray

Rabbits

Philippe Coudray

21

House painting

Philippe Coudray

Boomerang

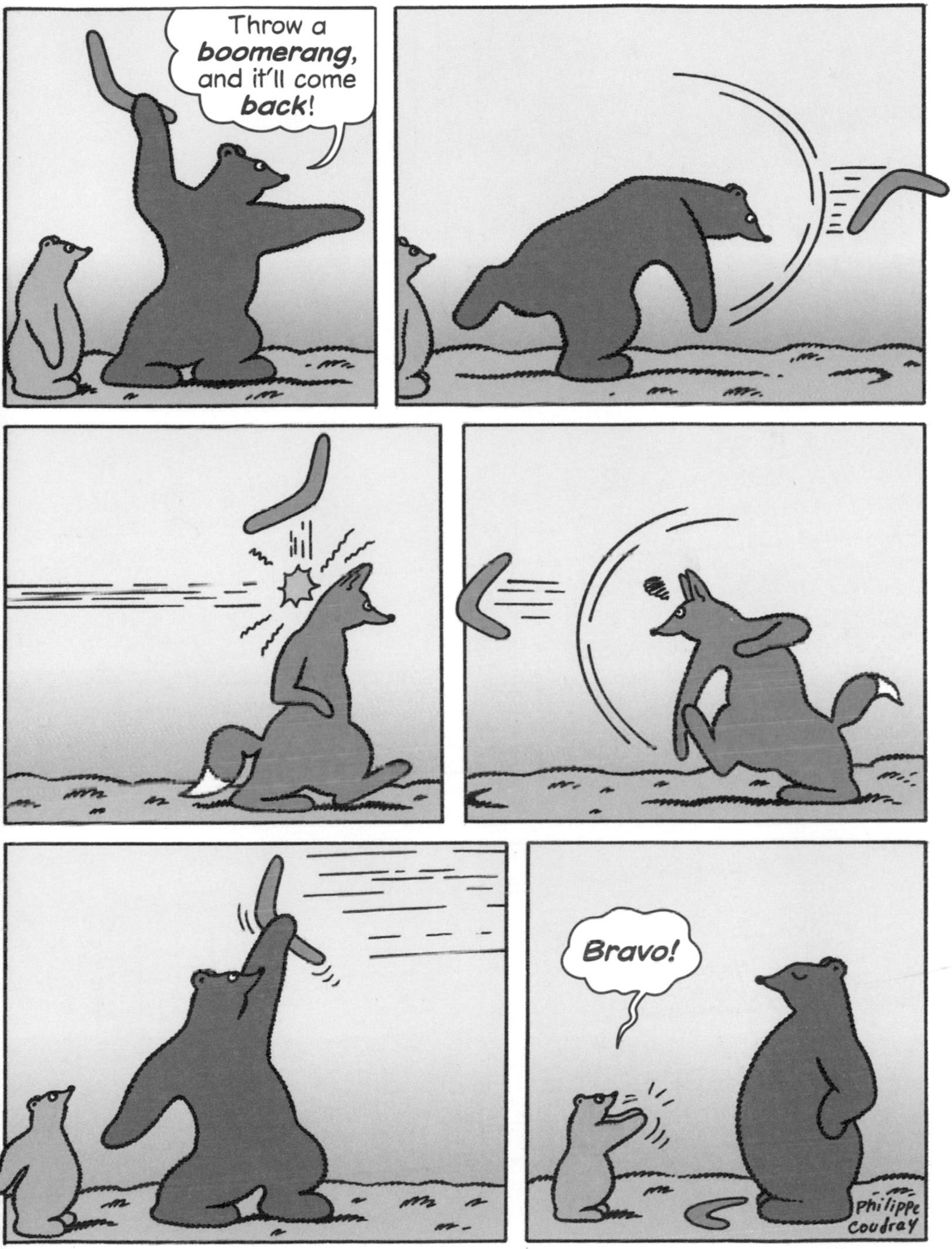
Throw a **boomerang**, and it'll come **back**!
Bravo!
Philippe Coudray

4 + 4 = 9

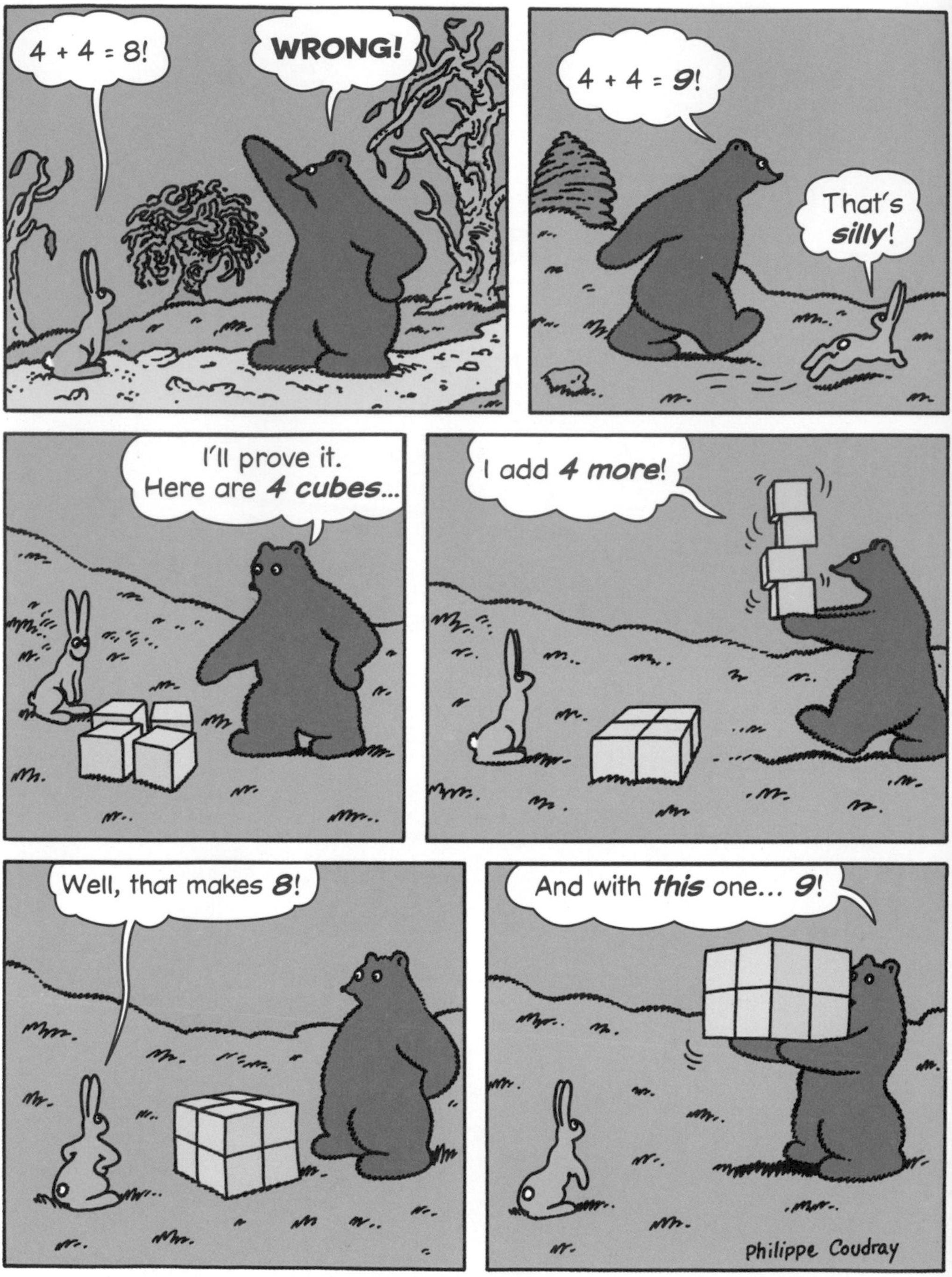
4 + 4 = 8!
WRONG!
4 + 4 = **9**!
That's **silly**!
I'll prove it. Here are **4 cubes**...
I add **4 more**!
Well, that makes **8**!
And with **this** one... **9**!
Philippe Coudray

Brute force

Philippe Coudray

The package

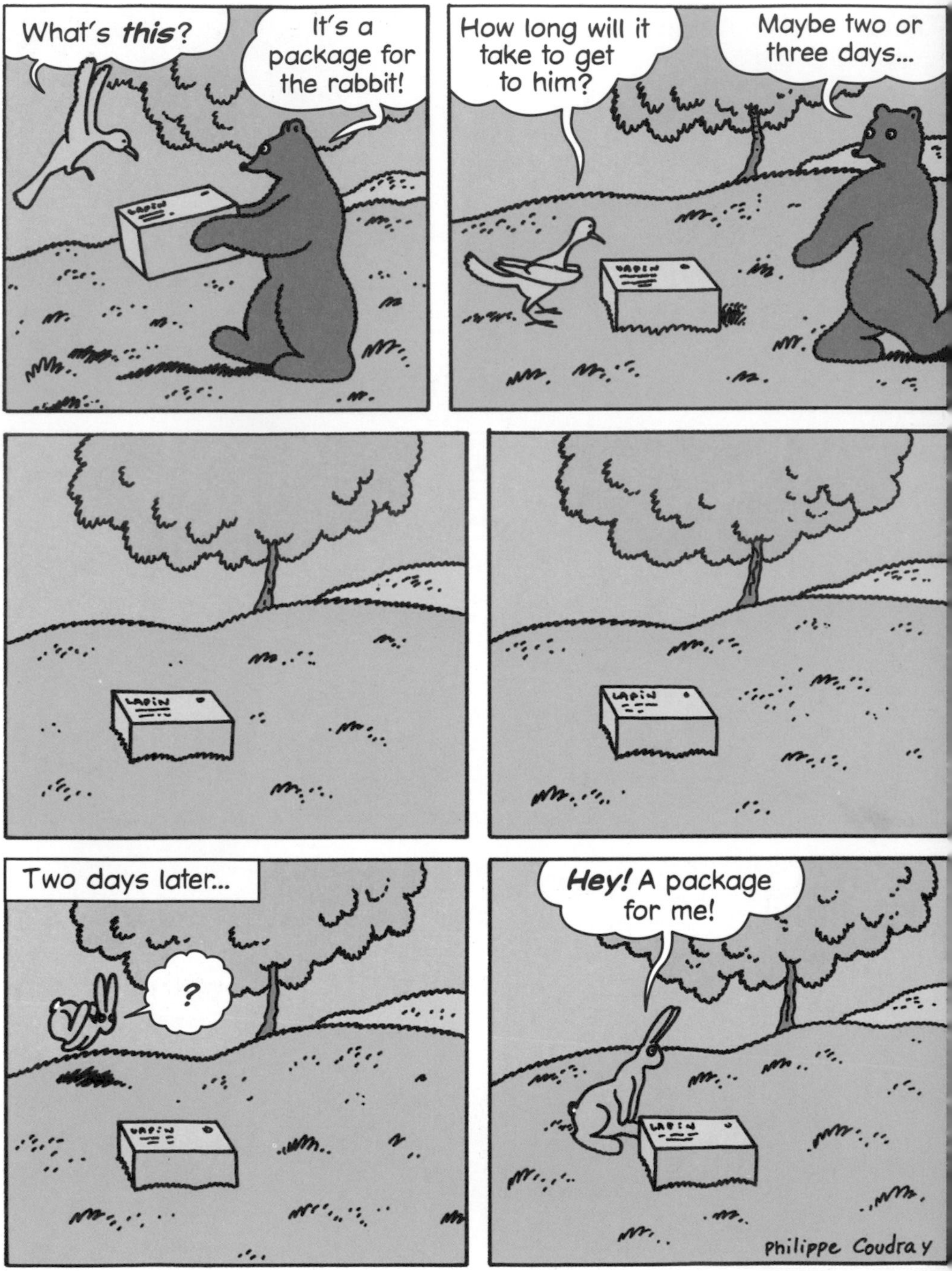
What's *this*?
It's a package for the rabbit!
How long will it take to get to him?
Maybe two or three days...
Two days later...
?
Hey! A package for me!
Philippe Coudray

River crossing

Philippe Coudray

27

Birdhouse

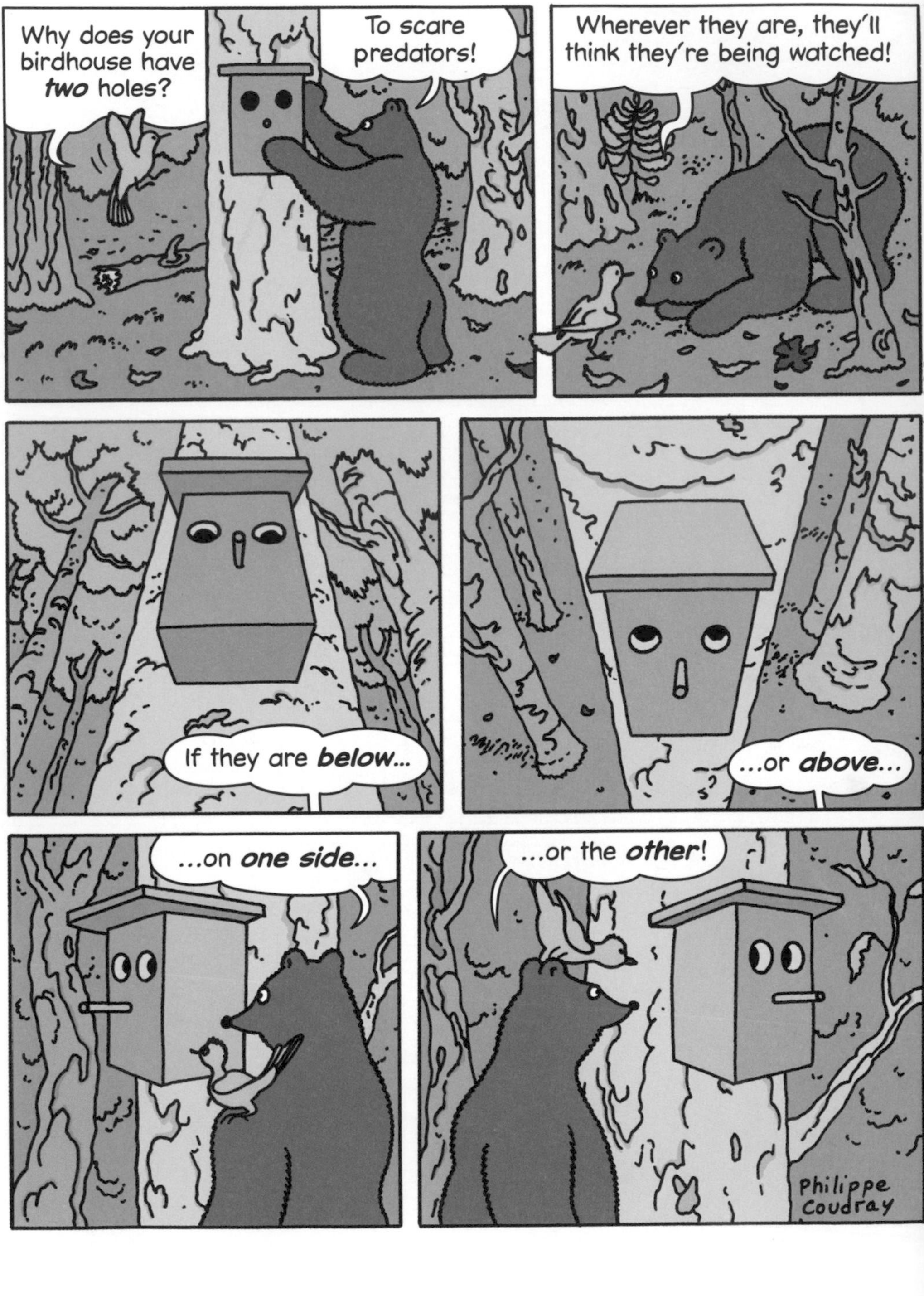
Why does your birdhouse have *two* holes?
To scare predators!
Wherever they are, they'll think they're being watched!
If they are *below*...
...or *above*...
...on *one side*...
...or the *other*!
Philippe Coudray

Stilts

Philippe Coudray

Bridging the gap

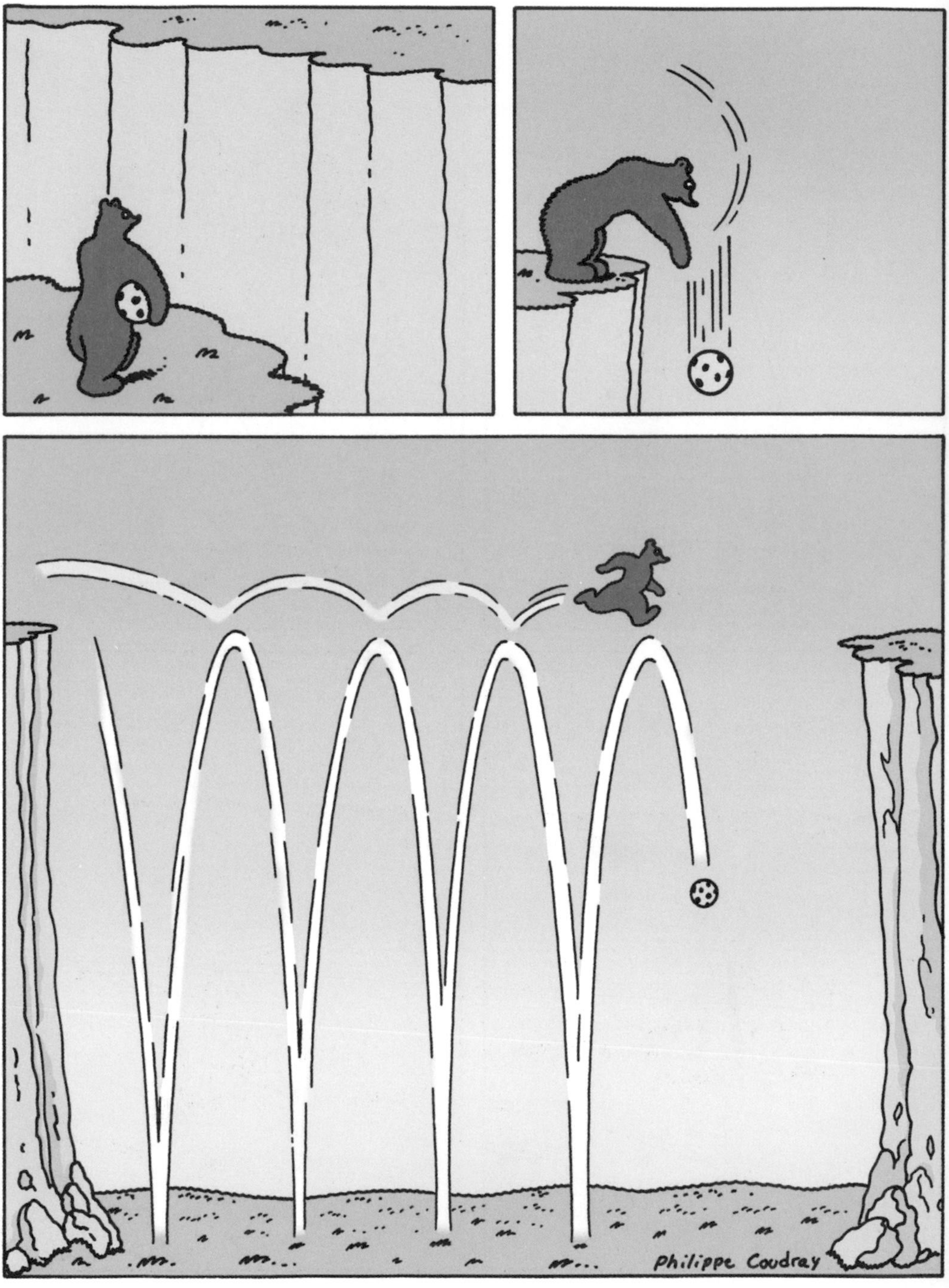
Philippe Coudray

Globe

philippe Coudray

The how-to book

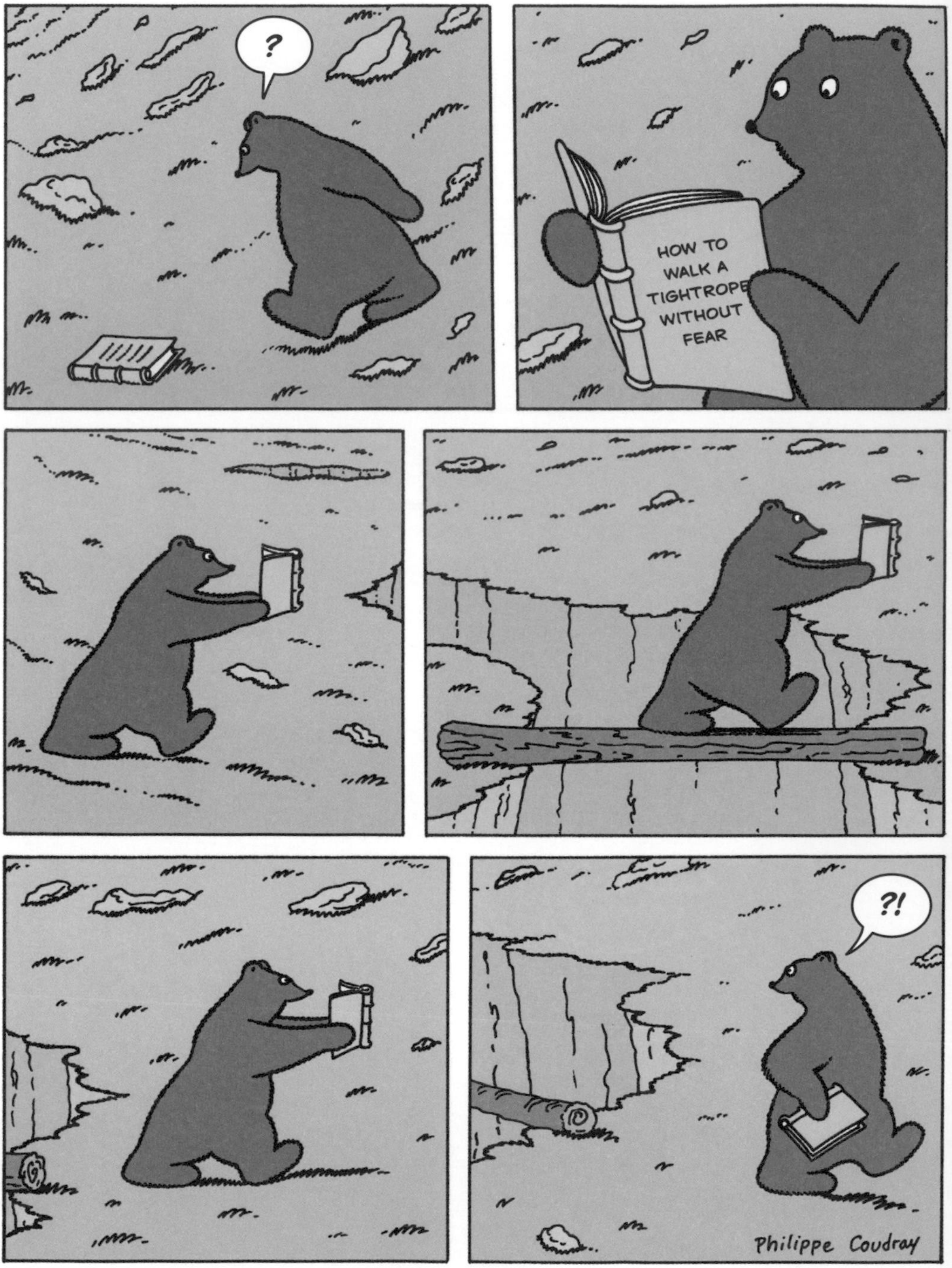
?
HOW TO WALK A TIGHTROPE WITHOUT FEAR
?!
Philippe Coudray

William Tell

Philippe Coudray

Parachute

Let's try parachuting!

Philippe Coudray

Stone fishing

Philippe Coudray

35

ABOUT THE AUTHOR

PHILIPPE COUDRAY loves drawing comics and working with his twin brother Jean-Luc, who is also a humorist. Philippe's books are favorites in the schools of France, his home country, where Benjamin Bear's French cousin, Barnabé, has won many prizes. The Benjamin Bear books have been nominated twice for the Eisner Award's Best Publication for Early Readers.

When he was younger, Philippe spent many of his family vacations in the mountains. He says, "I wanted to write a story about a bear because I love drawing the mountains where they live." In addition to his annual trip to Canada in search of Bigfoot, he enjoys creating stereoscopic images, and researching mythical creatures and other strange beasts.

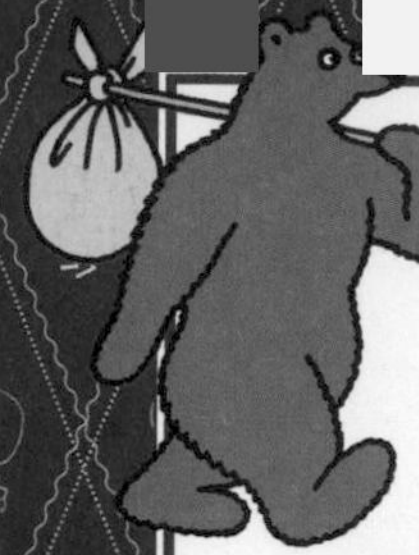

TIPS FOR PARENTS AND TEACHERS:

HOW TO READ COMICS WITH KIDS

Kids **love** comics! They are naturally drawn to the details in the pictures, which make them want to read the words. Comics beg for repeated readings and let both emerging and reluctant readers enjoy complex stories with a rich vocabulary. But since comics have their own grammar, here are a few tips for reading them with kids:

GUIDE YOUNG READERS: Use your finger to show your place in the text, but keep it at the bottom of the speaking character so it doesn't hide the very important facial expressions.

HAM IT UP! Think of the comic book story as a play and don't hesitate to read with expression and intonation. Assign parts or get kids to supply the sound effects, a great way to reinforce phonics skills.

LET THEM GUESS. Comics provide lots of context for the words, so emerging readers can make informed guesses. Like jigsaw puzzles, comics ask readers to make connections, so check a young audience's understanding by asking, "What's this character thinking?" (but don't be surprised if a kid finds some of the comics' subtle details faster than you).

TALK ABOUT THE PICTURES. Point out how the artist paces the story with pauses (silent panels) or speeded-up action (a burst of short panels). Discuss how the size and shape of the panels carry meaning.

ABOVE ALL, ENJOY! There is of course never one right way to read, so go for the shared pleasure. Once children make the story happen in their imagination, they have discovered the thrill of reading, and you won't be able to stop them. At that point, just go get them more books, and more comics.

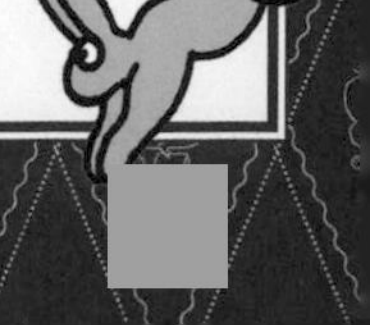